Plato Speaks

柏拉圖永恆名句

商務印書館

Plato Speaks 柏拉圖永恆名句

作　　者 ： 商務印書館編輯部
責任編輯 ： 黃家麗
封面設計 ： 涂慧
出　　版 ： 商務印書館（香港）有限公司
　　　　　　香港筲箕灣耀興道 3 號東滙廣場 8 樓
　　　　　　http://www.commercialpress.com.hk
發　　行 ： 香港聯合書刊物流有限公司
　　　　　　香港新界大埔汀麗路 36 號中華商務印刷大廈 3 字樓
印　　刷 ： 中華商務彩色印刷有限公司
　　　　　　香港新界大埔汀麗路 36 號中華商務印刷大廈 3 字樓
版　　次 ： 2016 年 7 月第 1 版第 1 次印刷
　　　　　　© 2016 商務印書館（香港）有限公司
　　　　　　ISBN 978 962 07 4546 1
　　　　　　Printed in Hong Kong

Contents 目錄

Knowledge is true opinion.

知識為真知灼見。

THEAETETUS

*The most important part of
education is proper training
in the nursery.*

教育最重要的，是自小獲得適當訓練。

LAWS

All the gold which is under or upon the earth is not enough to give in exchange for virtue.

屬世所有金銀財寶也不足以用來交換美德。

LAWS

4

A good decision is based on knowledge and not on numbers.

好決定建基於知識而非數字。

LACHES

The beginning is the most important part of the work.

起點是工作最關鍵的部份。

The Republic

Excess generally causes reaction, and produces a change in the opposite direction, whether it be in the seasons, or in individuals, or in governments.

過度一般引起對抗，會導致反方向的變化，無論出現於四季、個人或者政府層面。

THE REPUBLIC

The unexamined life is not worth living.

缺乏觀察體驗之生活沒有價值。

THE APOLOGY

... neither of us probably knows
anything that is really good,
but he thinks he has knowledge,
when he has not,
while I, having no knowledge,
do not think I have.

……誰也不知道甚麼是真正好的，
無知的人以為自己知道，我卻自知不明白。

THE APOLOGY

Do you know?

Plato's works cover a wide scope of themes: mathematics, sciences, nature, morals, and politics.

柏拉圖的作品涵蓋不同主題，
如數學、科學、自然、道德及政治。

*If it were necessary either to
do wrong or to suffer it,
I should choose to suffer
rather than do it.*

必要選擇做壞事或承受不做壞事
帶來的痛苦時，我應選擇受苦。

GORGIAS

For philosophy … if pursued in moderation and at the proper age, is an elegant accomplishment, but too much philosophy is the ruin of human life.

適度適時學習哲學是一種巧妙成就，
但過度就會變成人生的毀滅。

GORGIAS

Beauty is certainly a soft, smooth, slippery thing, and therefore of a nature which easily slips in and permeates our souls.

美有一份柔滑特質，
因此容易滲透我們的靈魂。

LYSIS

Do you know?

Plato never clearly spells out
the meaning of a dialogue for a reader.

柏拉圖從不明確向讀者闡述
其作品之意義。

Only a philosopher's mind
grows wings…

只有哲學家的心思會長出翅膀……

PHAEDRUS

Man is a prisoner who has no right to open the door of his prison and run away.

人是囚徒，無權打開囚室之門逃脫。

PHAEDRUS

The difficulty, my friends, is not in avoiding death, but in avoiding unrighteousness; for that runs faster than death.

我的朋友，困難不在於逃離死亡，
而在於逃離不公義，因為那比死亡奔馳更快。

Arguments, like men, are often pretenders.

爭論和人一樣，通常是偽裝者。

LYSIS

Do you know?

Plato's real name was Aristocles.

柏拉圖的原名為亞里斯多克勒斯。

…a man who is willing to value learning as long as he lives, will necessarily pay more attention to the rest of his life.

人若一生好學不倦，
會更在意餘生該怎樣過。

LACHES

Your silence gives consent.

你的沉默表示了默許。

CRATYLUS

Will not the good man, who says whatever he says with a view to the best, speak with a reference to some standard and not at random ...

好人講話不會隨意，總會依循某些準則……

GORGIAS

For to fear death, my friends,
is only to think ourselves wise
without really being wise, for it is
to think that we know what we do
not know.

我的朋友，
恐懼死亡僅是我們自以為聰明而非真正聰明，
這種恐懼源於以為知道所不知道的。

THE APOLOGY

Do you know?

Plato came from an aristocrat family.

柏拉圖來自一個貴族家庭。

*But of the heaven which
is above the heavens, what
earthly poet ever did or ever
will sing worthily?*

天外有天，俗世哪個詩人所吟詠的可與之相比？

PHAEDRUS

There is no such thing as a lovers' oath.

沒有愛盟這回事。

Symposium

At the touch of love
everyone becomes a poet.

愛使每個人當起了詩人。

SYMPOSIUM

Love is a serious mental disease.

愛是嚴重的精神病。

PHAEDRUS

No one is a friend to his friend who does not love in return.

若非彼此相愛，誰也不能成為誰的朋友。

LYSIS

Smooth is the way
that leads unto
wickedness

邪惡之路是平順的。

LAWS

Thinking is talking
to oneself.

思考是自言自語。

THEATETUS

Do you know?

"Plato" in Greek means "board".

"Plato" 於希臘文中有寬闊之意。

Courage is knowing what not to fear.

勇氣是明白無需畏懼甚麼。

LACHES

I exhort you also to take part in the great combat, which is the combat of life, and greater than every other earthly conflict.

我勸你參與這場大戰，就是人生實戰，
這比世上任何一場戰爭都要浩大。

GORGIAS

Courage is a kind of salvation.

勇氣是一種解救。

LACHES

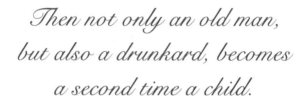

Then not only an old man,
but also a drunkard, becomes
a second time a child.

不僅是老年人，酒鬼也會再變成小孩一樣。

LAWS

Wealth is well known to be
a great comforter.

財富能夠為人帶來很大慰藉。

THE REPUBLIC

There are three classes of men; lovers of wisdom, lovers of honour, and lovers of gain.

世上有三類人：
愛智慧的人、愛名譽的人及愛利益的人。

THE REPUBLIC

They do certainly give very strange, and newfangled, names to diseases.

他們必定為疾病起奇特怪異的名字。

THE REPUBLIC

He who is of calm and happy nature will hardly feel the pressure of age, but to him who is of an opposite disposition, youth and age are equally a burden.

平靜喜樂的人幾乎不會感到衰老之壓力，
惟性情相反的人，青春和年邁同樣是負累。

THE REPUBLIC

Do you know?

When Plato was a child,
he learnt grammar and music.

柏拉圖童年學習文法和音樂。

There is no harm in
repeating a good thing.

持久行善有益無害。

LAWS

*No evil can happen to
a good man, either in life or
after death.*

好人在生前死後都不會遭遇邪惡。

To suffer the penalty of too much haste, which is too little speed.

太倉促會招致速度太慢之苦。

STATESMAN

Twice and thrice over
…good is it to repeat and
review what is good.

兩三次甚至更多⋯⋯
不斷行善、不斷反思甚麼是美善。

GORGIAS

*Good actions give strength
to ourselves and
inspire good actions in
others.*

好行為帶給我們力量，
也啟發別人有好行為。

CHARMIDES

The first and greatest victory
is to conquer yourself...

最大的勝利莫過於勝過自己⋯⋯

THE REPUBLIC

Poetry is nearer to vital truth than history.

詩比歷史更接近必不可缺的真理。

Ion

Do you know?

In Plato's youth,
he wrote plays and poetry.

在柏拉圖年青時期，他撰寫劇本及詩歌。

Any man may easily do harm, but not every man can do good to another.

傷害別人容易，但不是誰都能善待別人。

LAWS

As the builders say, the larger stones do not lie well without the lesser.

如建造者所言，沒有較小的石頭，
就沒有較大的石塊可紮根穩固。

Laws

He who is not a good servant will not be a good master.

一個人若不是好僕人，也不會是個好主人。

LAWS

Honesty is for the most part less profitable than dishonesty.

大多數情況下，誠實會比欺詐獲利較少。

THE REPUBLIC

Death is not the worst that can happen to men.

死亡並非人生最慘痛的經歷。

LAWS

Wonder is the feeling of the philosopher...

超凡奇妙是哲學家的感覺⋯⋯

THEAETETUS

Do you know?

Raphael painted Plato and
Aristotle in a famous composition known
as "The School of Athens".

藝術家拉斐爾創作了"雅典學院"。
畫中主角是柏拉圖與亞里士多德。

*Man never legislates, but destinies
and accidents, happening in all
sorts of ways, legislate in all sorts
of ways.*

人永不能定立甚麼，但命運和意外，
卻不斷以各種形式發生，決定了一切。

LAWS

Opinion is the medium between knowledge and ignorance.

見解是知識與無知之橋樑。

CHARMIDES

Do you know?

The first time that Plato and Socrates met each other was in a market.

柏拉圖與蘇格拉底是在一個市場內
初次見面的。

To do injustice is more disgraceful than to suffer it.

造成不公義比承受不公義之苦
更令人蒙羞。

GORGIAS

We do not learn; and what
we call learning is only a
process of recollection.

我們沒有學習，我們所謂的學習，
只不過是重溫記憶的過程。

Meno

Justice means minding one's own business and not meddling with other men's concerns.

公義是管好自己的事，不干涉別人的事。

THE REPUBLIC

Excess of liberty, whether it lies in state or individuals, seems only to pass into excess of slavery.

過度自由，不論在國家或個人層面，
似乎只會轉化為極度奴役。

THE REPUBLIC

Necessity... the mother of invention.

必要……乃發明之母。

THE REPUBLIC

The good is the beautiful.

善就是美。

LYSIS

Do you know?

Plato was a student of Socrates and
the teacher of Aristotle.

柏拉圖是蘇格拉底的學生，
也是亞里士多德的老師。

Better a little which is well done, than a great deal imperfectly.

寧可小事做好，勝過糟蹋大事。

THEAETETUS

If a man neglects education,
he walks lame to the end
of his life.

忽視教育的人，
終其一生會像跛子一樣。

TIMAEUS

We can easily forgive a child who is afraid of the dark; the real tragedy of life is when men are afraid of the light.

我們容易寬恕怕黑的小孩；
但人生真正的可悲，是人害怕光明。

DAY'S COLLACON

*Music is the movement of
sound to reach the soul for
the education of its virtue.*

音樂是聲音的流動，可觸動靈魂，
滋養它的美善。

STATESMAN

... too much cleverness and too much learning, accompanied with ill bringing-up, are far more fatal.

……太聰明和學識太多，
但教養欠奉是最致命的。

LAWS

Philosophy begins in wonder.

哲學始於驚奇感。

THEAETETUS

Do you know?

Plato served as a soldier in the
Peloponnesian War against Spart.

柏拉圖曾參與伯羅奔尼撒戰爭。

Wisdom alone is the science
of other sciences.

唯獨智慧是科學之中的科學。

CHARMIDES

... knowledge is the food of the soul.

……知識為靈魂之糧。

PROTAGORAS

$\mathcal{D}$o you know?

The Academy was forced
to close by the Roman Emperor,
Justinian, in an effort to suppress
the heresy of pagan thought.

羅馬帝皇查士丁尼以壓制異端思想為由，
下令關閉柏拉圖學院。

... the first and best of victories,
the lowest and worst of defeats
which each man gains or sustains
at the hands not of another, but of
himself.

……有首次大獲全勝，有最慘烈的失敗，
但勝負關鍵不在於別人，而在於自己。

LAWS

Knowledge which is acquired under compulsion obtains no hold on the mind.

遭強迫灌輸的知識不會長久。

THE REPUBLIC

Knowledge without justice
ought to be called cunning
rather than wisdom.

沒有公義的知識，是狡詐而非智慧。

MENEXENUS

The excessive increase of anything causes a reaction in the opposite direction.

任何事情做得過份，會引起反方向的對抗。

THE REPUBLIC

Do you know?

Socrates spoke in nearly all Plato's dialogues.

蘇格拉底幾乎出現在
所有柏拉圖對話作品中。

The direction in which education starts a man will determine his future in life.

教育方向的起點足以決定一個人的未來。

Do you know?

The students of The Academy were taught philosophy, political theory, and mathematics.

柏拉圖學院的學生學習哲學、
政治理論和數學。

Do you know?

The Republic and *Laws* marks Plato as a
founder of western political philosophy.

《理想國》與《法律篇》令柏拉圖被譽為
西方政治哲學始祖。

*To prefer evil to good is not in
human nature; and when a man
is compelled to choose one of
two evils, no one will choose the
greater when he might have
the less.*

喜惡拒善非人之常情，若被迫選擇兩種惡，
如能選那較小的惡，沒有人會選那較大的惡。

PROTAGORAS

Styles of music are never disturbed without affecting the most important political institutions.

若非影響到最重要的政治制度，
音樂絕不會受到干預。

THE REPUBLIC

Did you ever observe how imitations ... at length grow into habits and become a second nature, affecting body, voice, and mind?

你可有留意，模仿久而久之變為習慣，
變為第二本性，影響着肉身、言行及心智？

THE REPUBLIC

The real artist, who knew
what he was imitating, would
be interested in realities and
not in imitations…

真正的藝術家知道自己在模仿甚麼，
會關注真實，而非模仿物……

THE REPUBLIC

Do you know?

After Socrates died, Plato travelled across the Mediterranean region for 12 years.

蘇格拉底去世後，
柏拉圖遊歷地中海區域達十二年。

*Friends have all things
in common.*

朋友共通之處不計其數。

The poet is like a painter ...who will make a likeness of a cobbler though he understands nothing of cobbling.

詩人像畫家⋯⋯可以對補鞋一竅不通，
但塑造出活靈活現的補鞋匠。

THE REPUBLIC

And the excellence or beauty
or truth of every structure … is
relative to the use for which nature
or the artist has intended them.

每種構造的精妙美善⋯⋯
都相對於大自然或藝術家的意圖如何。

THE REPUBLIC

To a man full of questions
make no answer at all.

不必回應滿腹疑問的人。

DAY'S COLLACON

Are you not ashamed that you give your attention to acquiring as much money as possible ... and give no attention or thought to truth and understanding and the perfection of your soul?

難道你沒有為自己只顧賺錢……
沒思考或了解過自己靈魂的真相和
完美而羞愧嗎？

THE APOLOGY

Do you know?

After the execution of Socrates,
Plato gave up his political aspirations
and immersed himself in philosophy.

蘇格拉底被處死後，
柏拉圖放棄自己原有的政治抱負，
沉醉於哲學之中。

A work well begun is half ended.

好開始成就了工作的一半。

DAY'S COLLACON

*He seemeth to be most
ignorant that trusteth most
to his wit.*

最深信自己才智的人似乎是最無知的人。

DAY'S COLLACON

*Beauty of style and harmony
and grace and good rhythm
depend on simplicity.*

風格、和諧、優雅和韻律之美，
均來自簡約。

THE REPUBLIC

All who do evil and dishonorable things do them against their will.

一切作惡的無恥之徒，
做壞事時都違反了本身的意志。

PROTAGORAS

Wisdom always makes men fortunate.

智慧總是為人帶來幸運有利的條件。

EUTHYDEMUS

I am not given to finding fault, for there are innumerable fools.

我不是一個愛挑剔的人，
只不過愚人實在不計其數。

PROTAGORAS

Many men are loved by their enemies, and hated by their friends, and are the friends of their enemies, and the enemies of their friends.

許多人為敵人所喜愛，被他們的朋友憎厭，
是他們敵人的朋友，也是他們朋友的敵人。

LYSIS

 Do you know?

Plato is an educator.
He has established The Academy.

柏拉圖是位教育家。
他創辦了柏拉圖學院。

If a man can be properly said to love something, it must be clear that he feels affection for it as a whole, and does not love part of it to the exclusion of the rest.

人若真正喜愛某事物，沒有任何疑惑的是他對它有完整的喜愛，並非愛它某部份，而拒絕其餘部份。

THE REPUBLIC

Was not this ... what we spoke of as the great advantage of wisdom – to know what is known and what is unknown to us?

可不是這樣，我們所説智慧的最大好處，
是明白已知的事，也明白甚麼是未知的事？

CHARMIDES

105

The eyes ... are the windows of the soul.

眼睛是靈魂之窗。

PHAEDRUS

For all good and evil, whether in the body or in human nature, originates … in the soul, and overflows from thence, as from the head into the eyes.

所有善惡，不論是肉體或人性之內的，
都源自靈魂，從裏面湧流出去，
自頭腦湧進眼睛。

CHARMIDES

That's what education should be ... the art of orientation.

教育應該指引方向和基本態度。

THE REPUBLIC

There is in every one of us,
even those who seem to be most
moderate, a type of desire that is
terrible, wild, and lawless.

每個人裏面都有一種可怕的野性，

妄顧法紀的慾望，

連那些看似溫和的人也不例外。

THE REPUBLIC

Do you know?

Most of Plato's works
originated in his teaching
in The Academy.

柏拉圖大部份作品，
源於課堂上的對話。

If you are wise, all men will
be your friends and kindred,
for you will be useful.

如果你有智慧，
誰都想做你的朋友或志趣相投的夥伴，
那是因為你對他們有用。

LYSIS

For this ... is the great error
of our day in the treatment of
the human body, that physicians
separate the soul from the body.

醫治身體的最大錯誤，
就是醫生分開了靈魂和肉體。

CHARMIDES

False words are not only evil in themselves, but they infect the soul with evil.

虛假之言不僅是惡事，
也使靈魂遭受惡念的污染。

Do you know?

Plato never speaks in his own voice
in his dialogues,
except in *The Apology*.

柏拉圖沒有在他的對話作品中發聲，
除了在《申辯篇》之外。

There is great reason to hope
that death is good... either death
is a state of nothingness and utter
unconsciousness, or... there is a
change and migration of the soul
from this world to another.

死亡可望是好的⋯⋯
它可能是虛空無知覺的狀態⋯⋯
或是靈魂從今世轉移到另一個世界。

THE APOLOGY

Musical training is a more potent instrument than any other, because rhythm and harmony find their way into the inward places of the soul.

音樂訓練比任何方法強大有效，
因為節奏感、和諧均可觸動靈魂深處。

THE REPUBLIC

Tools which would teach men their own use would be beyond price.

教人明白自己有用之處的方法是無價寶。

THE REPUBLIC

... all things at the last be swallowed up in death?

……所有事物最終難免遭死亡吞滅？

PHAEDO

Do you know?

Most of Plato's works take
the form of a dialogue.

柏拉圖的作品大多使用對話形式。

The good are like one another, and friends to one another.

好人有相似的特質，彼此也能成為朋友。

LYSIS

Wealth is the parent of luxury and indolence, and poverty of meanness and viciousness, and both of discontent.

財富是奢華懶散之母，貧窮是刻薄敗壞之母，
兩者源於不知足。

THE REPUBLIC

The like is not the friend of the
like in as far as he is like; still the
good may be the friend of the good
in as far as he is good.

行為相似不等於是朋友；
但內心美善的人就有與其同心的朋友。

LYSIS

Plato's Works

柏拉圖名著

Before 387 B.C.E	The Apology 申辯篇
	Charmides 卡爾米德篇
	Gorgias 高爾吉亞篇
	Ion 伊安篇
	Laches 拉凱斯篇
	Lysis 呂西斯篇
	Protagoras 普羅泰戈拉篇
387-380 B.C.E.	Menexenus 美涅克塞努篇
	Meno 美諾篇
380-360 B.C.E.	Phaedo 斐多篇
	Symposium 會飲篇
	The Republic 理想國
	Cratylus 克拉梯樓斯篇
360-355 B.C.E.	Phaedrus 斐德若篇
	Theaetetus 泰阿泰德篇
	Timaeus 蒂邁歐篇
355-347 B.C.E.	Laws 法律篇
	Statesman 政治家篇

Plato's Epitaph

柏拉圖墓誌銘

Star-gazing Aster,

would I were the skies,

To gaze upon thee with a thousand eyes.

願我化作夜空，

以閃亮的眼眸遙望看星的你。